SAM DOWLING
Is a Dublin-born playwright. He has written and produced nearly thirty plays or small-cast versions of classics for Praxis Theatre Laboratory. His subject-matter has ranged from Irish history through the lives of writers and artists to re-working of themes from the Greek myths. His play about the Brontës (co-written with Andrea Bird) has had three productions in Tokyo.
For more detail see playwrights' database at www.doollee.com

PRAXIS THEATRE LABORATORY is an experimental theatre which seeks its direction from the actors' response to the work. No-one takes on a separate role as director. We particularly value images conjured in rehearsal, and intuitive and emotional rather than intellectual or technical evaluation. We try to fix as little as possible and each performance retains an element of improvisation.
Founded by Sam Dowling as the in-house company at The Tabard in West London from 1984, in 1990 we left to pursue more experimental goals. We opened a small theatre space in County Roscommon, Ireland in 1999 and have toured UK, USA, Ireland, Belgium, Netherlands, Ukraine and Poland.

First performed in July 2001 as part of Boyle Arts Festival in Co. Roscommon with this cast:

MAUD GONNE McBRIDE..Maria Straw

W. B. YEATS...John Lawler

Designed by Claire Harvey

IRISH PLAYS AND OTHERS BY SAM DOWLING IN PRINT OR IN THE PIPELINE

RIVERMAN [Walter Greaves, naïf painter, rise and fall.]
CAULDRON OF BRONTËS [Genius siblings.]
A SEASON IN HELL [Wild poets Rimbaud and Verlaine.]
MOUNTAIN [Life-changing encounters]
RENEWAL [Site-specific version of MOUNTAIN]
TROJAN WOMEN
BIRTH OF THE BEAST [Northern Ireland.]
BIG FELLA! [Michael Collins.]
ALLEGIANCE [IRA in London.]
ANTIGONE
THE FLAME AND THE STONE [Yeats and Maud Gonne.]
VIRGIN OF NOTTING HILL [Sexual problems.]
ORESTEIAN TRILOGY
LOVELOST [Abuse]
RED COUNTESS GREEN CROW [Markievicz and O'Casey]
HA! HA! HA! [Improvisations on Coward and Shakespeare.]

AND SMALL-CAST VERSIONS OF THESE CLASSICS;

THE CENCI
IMPORTANCE OF BEING EARNEST
CHERRY ORCHARD
THREE SISTERS
HEDDA GABLER
WHEN WE DEAD AWAKEN
HAMLET
MACBETH
ANTONY AND CLEOPATRA
THE TEMPEST

IRISH PLAYS AND OTHERS Volume 10

Maud Gonne and W.B.Yeats
THE FLAME AND THE STONE

A play by Sam Dowling

2000-2001

Sam Dowling
85 Haddo House
Haddo Street
LONDON SE10 9SE

E-mail praxis.lab@ntlworld.com

Published by Lulu 2007

www.lulu.com

ISBN 978-1-84753-765-2

DRAMATIS PERSONAE

W. B. YEATS

MAUD GONNE McBRIDE

The play is outside linear time, and covers almost the entire period of the characters' relationship

The production in 2001 included original slides drawn by Clare Harvey. The slides were some abstract and some realistically related to the action.

Part One

[The Union Jack flies over Ireland.]

GONNE
It wasn't your father I came to see

YEATS
My sister Lilly says
You never took your eyes off me for one second
She didn't like it

GONNE
Sizing you up
For Ireland

YEATS
You frightened my father with your talk of dynamite and guns

GONNE
His portrait of O'Leary is magnificent

YEATS
It's not quite finished
He never quite finishes anything

GONNE
You seem reasonably well finished

YEATS
You have the most disturbing way of touching me

GONNE
And you, Willie wagtail
Do you finish things ?

YEATS
I'm better at starting things
That much from my father

GONNE
Our meeting started something

YEATS
I hope so

GONNE
For Ireland

YEATS
I love you Maud

GONNE
I love you Willie
You're like a brother to me

YEATS
That moment you walked into the house in Bedford Park
I was physically shocked
I knew beyond a shadow of doubt
My entire future was standing within arms reach
....
Kiss me Maud Gonne

GONNE
As a child
Howth Head was my Himalayas
We had that house just over there
My father would carry me on his shoulders
When he was home on leave
Or I'd come on my own
If I could give my nanny the slip
Up here with the gulls... wheeling out over the rocks
Children can fly you know
That's the Three Rock Mountain over there... Big Sugarloaf... Little Sugarloaf... Bray Head
I knew them all intimately
Flew over them a hundred times

YEATS
Next time I'll fly with you
Two white birds on the foam of the sea

GONNE
Put that in a poem for me

YEATS
I'm already writing a play for you
About a noble woman
The Countess Kathleen
Who sells her soul to save her people

GONNE
An Irishwoman sells her soul
And saves her people

YEATS
She may be squandering her precious soul

GONNE
I hope you don't expect me to play your Countess

YEATS
Marry me Maud

GONNE
No thank you

YEATS
Because I have no money

GONNE
It's not money Willie

YEATS
I borrowed ten shillings from O'Leary to come out here today

GONNE
I pay my own way

YEATS
You don't know what it's like being poor

GONNE
You don't
One day up in Donegal
I followed Colonel Olphert's agent around his estates
On this old nag I hired in Gweedore
Him and a dozen bailiffs... fearsome ruffians

Evicting tenants all day
That's what they did for a day's work
Six evictions in one day
I kicked up a most awful row every time he tried to throw people out
Ranting and raving for all I was worth
Eventually we had about fifty men standing between the bailiffs and the third cottage
I do believe he would have shot me dead if I weren't a woman
Willie the people there think I'm some kind of an apparition
The woman of the Sidhe they say
I suppose I do look a bit incongruous
In my sealskin coat
Actually it's quite ancient
I got it for my coming-out in Dublin Castle
What I wanted to say about poverty was...
When we came to the cottage
The windows and door had all been built up with masonry... on the inside
And just a whisp of smoke coming from the chimney
So we knew the family were inside
Our men were ready for anything
Eventually the bailiffs turned away
And two big chaps started demolishing the stonework blocking up the opening inside
Suddenly one of them turned and said
' Go on now Miss...you won't want to be seeing what's in here...'
I ran to the door and....
Willie... the little family... husband wife and two wee girls of three or four...
Were all lying.... their arms round each other
Every one of them thin as skeletons
And the fire was still burning
But they were dead

Every last one of them
And not a potato or a cabbage let alone a hen or a cow left about their little farm

YEATS
The Land Acts have put an end to all that

GONNE
For the strong farmers
Meanwhile an entire underclass is being liquidated

YEATS
I'm inclined to agree with O'Leary
He says the land question is obscuring the national vision
In the long run the Irish people will be liberated by their culture
Not by hanging landlords

GONNE
I see no reason why one should hold back the other

YEATS
Your father isn't a landlord

GONNE
Neither is yours

YEATS
The Butler side of the family have the remnants of an estate in County Kilkenny
You're afraid to marry me in case the tenants hang the pair of us

GONNE
One thing my father taught me

Never to be afraid
Not to fear anything
Even death

YEATS
Only marriage

GONNE
I'm not afraid of marriage Willie
Like parsnips
I'm not afraid of them but I never eat them

YEATS
They're very good for you

GONNE
They make me ill

YEATS
It makes me ill having you so close to me
And you won't let me kiss you

GONNE
I didn't say that
[SHE allows a kiss on the cheek.]
That's enough young man

YEATS
I expect you'd marry me if I weren't a poor poet

GONNE
Poets should not marry

YEATS
Be my lover

GONNE
Stop harassing me

YEATS
You are devoid of all womanly feelings

GONNE
That's right
[Hugs and kisses him but not on the mouth.]

YEATS
Oh god !

GONNE
Willie I have to go back to Paris urgently

YEATS
I'll come with you

GONNE
No

YEATS
O'Leary will lend me the money

GONNE
It's a kind of secret thing

YEATS
A man

GONNE
I told you I'm involved in a revolutionary group

YEATS
So am I

GONNE
A French group
Oath-bound
I shouldn't even say that much

[HE sees she has a gun.]

YEATS
What do you need a gun for ?

GONNE
I've been recalled urgently

YEATS
I need to know what you're doing

GONNE
....

YEATS
Answer me...please

GONNE
......

YEATS
All right

GONNE
.....

[Kisses him lightly]

I'll telegraph when I'm coming back, my dear
In a week or two

[EXIT.]

YEATS
Maud !

[Light change.
MAUD is in Paris with her child, Georges
and her lover Lucien Millevoye.].]

GONNE
My darling pet !
Such a bad mother aren't I ?
Leaving you all on your own
You'll have to get well now for Mama
I brought you all kinds of lovely things from Dublin
Toy soldiers and a little farm
With cows and horses and chickens
And a little pair of blue booties cos you're starting to walk for Mama
And I'll never leave you on your own ever ever ever...
And I won't take my eyes off you again not for one second
Ever !
.....
NURSE ! He's stopped breathing ! HE'S STOPPED BREATHING !
LUCIEN ! LUCIEN ! QUICK !
OH NO NO NO NO NO NO !

[Light change.
MAUD is back in Dublin.]

YEATS
You said you'd be back in a week

GONNE
Please
I came as soon as I could

YEATS
I was worried sick

It's been nearly three months

GONNE
Things went terribly wrong

YEATS
You look awful

GONNE
I feel washed out

YEATS
What did that gang want of you ?

GONNE
Who ? Oh that...

YEATS
Don't tell me if you don't want to
......
You know Parnell's coffin came in with you on the Mailboat ?

GONNE
Of course
Willie I didn't see you at the funeral
What a turn-out ! The biggest crowd ever seen on the streets of Dublin

YEATS
I hate public funerals

GONNE
Ha !

You're not expected to enjoy them you know
I suppose you think private funerals are a bit of fun

YEATS
The Irish turn every public funeral into a political stunt

GONNE
It was no political stunt !
Not a priest or a bishop in sight
This was the real thing
The ordinary people coming out to grieve their murdered king

YEATS
Parnell died of despair

GONNE
He was murdered by English agents

YEATS
Take that with a grain of salt my dear

GONNE
You are a great man for standing up for the police

YEATS
You're obsessively prejudiced against them

GONNE
They're there to protect the haves against the have-nots
I'm on the side of the have-nots

YEATS
Look at yourself Maud

A walking contradiction
Sure we can work for the liberation the education of the masses
But don't pretend you're one of the great unwashed because you're not and never will be

GONNE
Not unwashed maybe
But Willie I am one of the mob
Always there at their heart's core
And you're not
And we scare you to death
Because you are bourgeois and afraid of your own annihilation
And we of the mob fear nothing

YEATS
Perhaps you're right

GONNE
A thing happened out there in Glasnevin cemetery
That could only happen to such a multitude
That's why you should have been there
To chronicle it
Your archetypes there in the flesh
We filled every corner of the cemetery
Maybe half a million people
Hearts beating as one body
It was near dusk with a threatening leaden sky
Someone lifted the first shovelful of earth to fill in Parnell's grave
I swear on the instant the earth thudded on to the wood of the coffin
The clouds parted like a curtain
A swathe of blue sky appeared over our heads
And across it shot a great comet or shooting star or don't know what
And I heard a voice

In my head or in the crowd or from the blue sky
But this voice was clear as a bell to me
'Life out of death
Life out of death eternally !'

YEATS
It has brought back the light into your eyes
I thank God or the ghost of Parnell for that

GONNE
....
Something quite shattering happened in France

YEATS
.....

GONNE
....
I took a little boy into my house
An orphan
Georges
He was just nineteen months

YEATS
When you took him in

GONNE
When he died on me
Oh God ! I... we all loved him so much
Like....

YEATS
One of your own

GONNE
Yes
Meningitis

YEATS
No

GONNE
I couldn't know could I ?
I didn't leave him for one minute once I knew
The bird of death was pecking at the window
Like it always does in our family
That's when I knew and I sent for every doctor I could find
But they couldn't help him

YEATS
You should have children of your own Maud
You'd be a wonderful mother

GONNE
You said I had none of the womanly virtues
It's true
I haven't the right to be a mother
I want too much out of life
But the strange thing is Willie
I really do love children
....
Do you believe in reincarnation ?

YEATS
Of course

GONNE
Maybe I'll get another chance to see little Georges
I'll keep a sharp lookout for him

YEATS
George Russell says you can be reincarnated in your own family
Are the little boy's parents alive ?

GONNE
Vanished from the face of the earth
He was found on the steps of Sacre Coeur
'Father and mother unknown'
I have his poor birth certificate

[Light change
Back in France at Samois-sur-Seine.]

GONNE
Lucien.. Get up will you dear
We're going down to Georges's grave
To make a baby
.....
I said to make another baby
I'm quite serious
....
No ! Down there
I've taken some excellent advice
It seems a child can be reincarnated quite quickly
In the same family
Same father and mother
Ha ha ! Non mon cher pas ici !
We are to make love in his little tomb
On the what-do-you-call-it... ? Stone thing

Yes sarcophagus... or under it if you wish
That's why he's embalmed you know
I knew I'd get him back somehow
And we have to do it before his little soul leaves the area
....
Mmm I love you too Lucien Millevoye !

[Light change.]

Part Two

[Dublin.]

GONNE

The English have a peculiar talent for dehumanising Irish prisoners
O'Leary had marked my card about taking someone with me
Portland Jail... more like Portland Hell
They won't let the prisoners talk about anything
Their injuries treatment politics
I had this journalist-illustrator come with me so we could say to each other
What we wanted to say to the prisoners
Eight of them one by one
We were in a cage... like you'd see in a circus
And near it they had another cage for the prisoner
Between them a warder sitting holding a Service revolver at the ready
Across his knee
And the poor devils were shunted in and out one by one
In their clowns' outfit of yellow with black broad-arrows
The fourth man we saw
Peter O'Callaghan
Had lost one eye and the other was visibly rotting in his head
His body a walking skeleton
Peter tried to tell us about the eyes
The warder shouted and said he would take him back to his cell
Peter clung to the bars and I stopped him before the warder could hit him with his gun
I said... 'Peter ! I know exactly what happened to your eyes
And don't worry: you're going to be released within six months !'
And we talked away to each other the artist and I
Giving away as much news as we could
I knew us just being there was helping some way

We wanted another man to tell us what had happened to his cell-mate Dr Gallagher
The Amnesty Association had a report he'd gone insane
But this poor chap had entirely lost the ability to talk in any coherent way
What had they done to the two men in that cell ?
The strangest thing of all was this
I heard myself saying to each of the prisoners
You'll be out in six months or a year or nine months...something different for each of them
I couldn't help it
My journalist friend said 'That's cruel... they're all on life sentences'
He was wrong... the work started to pay off right away and releases came exactly as I had spoken them
Six months nine months a year. Whatever.
Sometimes miracles are no more than the reward for hard graft

YEATS

.....

Will you have time to do a bit of a miracle for me ?
That's what's needed to save the Library of Ireland
From my enemies

GONNE

Dr Sigerson isn't your enemy
Himself and Gavan Duffy don't see everything on the lofty plain you do
That doesn't make them your enemies

.....

Willie, I really don't think I have the physical strength to finish the Library lectures
Dr Sigerson says I need a complete rest

Would you mind very much if I put them on the back burner for a while ?

YEATS

That's entirely up to you

GONNE

I suppose now you'll be counting me among your enemies

YEATS

You know how I count you
Eventually I should like to set up an Irish mystical union
You would be central to the idea
Literary mystical political

GONNE

In the West of Ireland I feel really strange talking libraries to them
We should be teaching them how to make bullets
There's nothing wrong with your work Willie
Which is to write poetry
It is of the utmost importance
But my work is on another level
You may find a way of uniting them but I can't see it

YEATS

I can
It's beginning to happen
The reviews for the Countess Kathleen were ecstatic

GONNE

You please the reviewers who are men of your own class
The mass of Catholic Irish peasants
Don't want their religion brushed aside like an old wives' tale

Neither do their priests
Archbishop Walsh doesn't think much of your Countess Kathleen

YEATS
The Irish peasant carries my entire mythology round in his head
Without even knowing it
The bishops may sense that

GONNE
To tell you the truth
I don't much care for the bold countess myself

YEATS
To tell you the truth
I don't care much for a lot of your politics
They veer perilously close to the lowest common Nationalist denominator

GONNE
That's the price of being one of the mob Willie
I tell you what I do like in the Countess volume is that poem 'Apologia...'

YEATS
I hope I wasn't pandering to your agenda
You have such a talent for the occult work
So receptive

GONNE
The prisoners have first call on me
But I desperately want to do more of the mystical work with you
I try to travel to you every night in my sleep or in the half-sleep
You know that and you must tell me if you're seeing anything

I keep a notebook and jot things down even in the middle of the night
I've been using chloroform which works for me
But I think I was getting a bit ...you know...addicted in fact
So I've gone back on the hashish
The results are less spectacular

YEATS
I'm the same
Not chloroform... mescal
But it catches me here and I can't breathe
It frightens me in case I can't come back sometime
Though I'm getting to all kinds of archetypal characters
So in a way it's worth it
A lot of them are Celtic including this Druidic guide or something
I think when you and I work together
With the extraordinary energy we two generate... the hashish is enough
But it takes time
And you're always rushing back and forth to Paris
Back and forth like a fiddler's elbow
If you were my wife
I wouldn't let you mess around with politics at all

GONNE
Which is another reason I never shall be your wife
Or anyone else's

YEATS
I wouldn't let you entertain my enemies
Ply them with tea and expensive cigarettes

GONNE
I never to turn away a dynamiter democrat

Revolutionist or constitutionalist
Or a poet
So long as they are working for Ireland

YEATS
I wish you were a little more discriminating

GONNE
That's wishing I were someone else

YEATS
Why are you so discriminating about whom you marry ?

GONNE
I tell you this William Butler Yeats
Ireland will thank me one day
For not marrying you
And if I'm wrong about that
Perhaps Ireland will thank you for not marrying me

YEATS
You expect me to spend my life writing doggerel to woo you
And go down to a poet's grave nursing my eternal virginity

GONNE
Aw poor Willie are you still a virgin ?

YEATS
Are you ?

GONNE
What a rude question !

YEATS
I hear so many vile rumours about you

GONNE
In Dublin I hear rumours about everyone
Including you
The latest is that you procured an abortion for me
In a certain side street in Rathmines to be precise
And that you supervised it personally
Do you think there might be any truth in it Willie ?

YEATS
I didn't say I gave them any credence

GONNE
An active independent woman is what they can't give credence to
Well they had better get bloody used to it
And so had you
You don't own me Willie and never will
Don't make me some big thing in your life because it won't work
I want to be your good friend
I want to work with you on the mystical thing on the nationalist thing on your poetry
And all the stories and poetry of the other patriot writers
But you have to draw some kind of line between all that and your sexual needs

YEATS
It's hard to draw that line Maud

GONNE
So be it then
But drawn it must be

YEATS
I love you

GONNE
Use it in your work
If you need a wife Ireland is full of pretty girls
If you need a mistress just open your eyes
Not in my direction
Florence Farr obviously fancies you
Olivia Shakespear undresses you shamelessly with those big blue eyes of hers
As soon as you come into the room
......
I'm going to Paris to get my strength back
So I can drive the English out of Ireland

YEATS
You're English

GONNE
You are
Or worse
Pollexfen
What kind of a name is that ?

[EXEUNT to a separate spaces]

YEATS
Devon
Maybe Celtic
The Yeats were Norman stock
De Butler

...
I must have said something to drive her away
Maybe she's right
As a poet I can see the value of unrequited love
That doesn't make it any easier
Florence Farr ....mmmm
Virginity really is a bit disgraceful at my age
And an artist

GONNE
Oh !
Julien I think I'm going into labour
I'll send for the midwife after dinner
....
No I'm fine
Excited
Can you imagine if it really is little Georges coming back to us ?
He'd be nearly five now if...
You'll have to start again my pet
It's like Snakes And Ladders... ' Go back to Start ! Lose one turn !'
Oh !
Julien ask Marie to go for the midwife right away !
And tell her I shan't bother with dinner

YEATS[in London]
Mrs Shakespear is so beautiful
And sympathetic
As much as told me she's going to make me her lover
If I get a place of my own
Grrr !
Which I have every hope of doing before too long
I was planning a little tête-à-tête here in Symonds's place which might eh...

GONNE [in France]
Isn't she sweet ?
Iseult
I'm not at all sure she's a reincarnation of my Georges
It doesn't seem to matter so much now
She's just ravishing
Babababa Ba!
I could eat you little Iseult !
......
No It's quite all right Marie
I'll put her to bed

YEATS [in London]
A bit like a French farce actually
Though it didn't seem funny at the time
She was to come for tea
Symonds safely overnight in Surrey somewhere
I was a bit short of cash as usual
Not sure that Mrs Shakespear would turn up
So I didn't buy any cakes or things until she actually arrived
I excused myself and slipped out to the bakery down the street
For some goodies

GONNE [in France]
I excused myself and went to talk to the maid
No idea why
When I came back there you were Willie
In among my friends leg crossed one over the other
Cup of tea balanced on knee
I spoke to you of course
No answer
Everyone looking at me strangely

Till I realised only I could see you
Though you were quite ...solid
Ha ! As solid as you ever are
And I asked you to come back to me later

YEATS [in London]
To cut a long story short
What do I do ? I forget my key...lock myself out
Mrs Shakespear waiting here for her cream buns and whatever
Kettle now hopelessly off the boil
Me three floors down on the doorstep with the buns
After about half an hour the man next door comes along and lets me up the stairs
Out on his roof in through Symonds's attic
In some disarray the cream buns a little the worse for wear
Frighten the daylights out of the delectable Mrs Shakespear... Olivia
Hat and coat on and was halfway down the stairs before I stopped her
The afternoon never quite recovered its promise
The poet's virginity remained excruciatingly intact

GONNE [in France]
That night I went out of my body to be with you
And we met
Astrally
We walked again through the furze and rocks on Howth Head
Like that other time
We held hands and were a bit sad
And the birds were silent
Not flying over the sea and rocks
The gulls were all asleep and silent
And I thought
I'm here because you need me

YEATS [in London]
Not for long
Olivia was my new muse
My obsession with Maud a thing of the past
Olivia Shakespear drew good work out of me
Much good poetry
'He bids his beloved be at rest'...'Travail of Love'... 'He gives his beloved certain Rhymes'
She drew other things out of me
Always with great tenderness
As from a child
And at last we were real lovers
And I was no longer a child with her
And hardly ever thought of Maud

GONNE [in France]
That's why I came back to you
Because I knew you needed me

YEATS [in London]
....
What ? Oh I was just thinking of an old friend
....
Yes she wrote to me a couple of times
....
Just mundane stuff
Raising money for the Treason-Felony prisoners
She's very active in the Amnesty Association
...
No there was never anything like that between us
Just a mutual interest in Ireland
And the occult

GONNE [in France]
When the birds were silent

YEATS [in London]
Excuse me

YEATS [in the same space as GONNE]
She could always see into my mind
She saw your image there
And was gone
And you are back
And I am content

GONNE
I never intended coming between

YEATS
Thoroughly unhappy and in love again

GONNE
More mature
Coming into your own at last
Plays in the West End
Books doing well
A mistress at last
Two or is it three ?

YEATS
You're laughing at me

GONNE
I always wanted you to find the women you needed
...

Who is this lady from Galway ?

YEATS
Lady Gregory
Very distinguished

GONNE
I know when you say distinguished you mean rich

YEATS
Do I ?
Ha ha ! Perhaps I do
That's a bit careless of me
Very distinguished and rich

GONNE
You are a proper snob Willie Yeats

YEATS
She is making an excellent collection of folk tales
And has a fairyland of an estate
Woods a lake with many wild swans
We are going to collaborate on something for the theatre

GONNE
How is she on the national question ?

YEATS
She has no politics...she's a liberal unionist
With an extraordinary love of Ireland and everything Irish

GONNE
No sense of outrage

YEATS
Absolutely not

GONNE
An untenable position !

YEATS
Eminently tenable
I've seen the same thing in the best of my Sligo relations
There are two sets of Irish mythologies
The great and ancient Celtic mysteries
Or the myths of the music-hall sentimentalists
The tear and the shamrock school
Lady Gregory submits only to the former
You dear Maud can be seduced by either

GONNE
This is how I'll lose you

YEATS
How could you lose me ?
No more than I could lose the shape you've laid on me

GONNE
Each on the other
....
I look in my mirror and hate what I see
In the mirror of your eyes Willie
I see a woman with a claim to ...wholeness
Some kind of beauty even
That shape you've laid on me

YEATS

Maud I have the most wonderful idea
I was up in Roscommon with Douglas Hyde
The entire landscape from Boyle to Sligo is one enormous outdoor cathedral
The footprints of the druids in very field
From the Bricklieves right across to Meabh's cairn on Knocknarea
Twenty five miles or more
Then on Lough Key outside Boyle we found this island with a castle
It is habitable and can be rented
So I have a plan
I'm sure the gods want us to do this thing together

GONNE

I had dream about a castle
And a kind of church where I was a priestess...

YEATS

That's it ! You and I are the priesthood
We are to rediscover the Irish mysteries
Through meditation and ritual
And the best of the young men of Ireland will come there
To learn and to prepare themselves for the liberation of Ireland
We must find the rituals and the invocations that we need to take there
To our Castle Of Heroes...that's what I call it
It can all be done without great expense or anything like that
I quizzed Hyde about it... it is possible to live far cheaper than in Dublin

GONNE

I would have to keep the connections with Paris and the Dublin things

YEATS

Oh... would you ?

[THEY part.
He to Lady Gregory
she to her child.]

YEATS

I have a profound interest in the mystical side of Ireland Lady Gregory
In spiritual things
In fairies though unlike Russell
I rarely see them
But above all I remain a sceptic
Always prepared to discover there is nothing spiritual beyond the mystery of our own tribal memories
Maud Gonne on the other hand believes implicitly in every god ghoul and hobgoblin in the country
I venture to say that if the true extent of her faith in the supernatural were known
Miss Gonne would be locked away as stark raving mad
[Laughter]
In politics she is of the right and the left simultaneously
Internationally
In France she is part of the revolutionary right
In Dublin the revolutionary left
She has joined The Irish Republican Socialist Party
Led by a young Scot called James Connolly
Who proposes to free Ireland with the help of half a dozen unemployed labourers
And three Corporation clerks
Sorry... two
One of them has deflected to a rival and equally absurd revolution
In the making by equally absurd people

[Laughter]
Here I must confess that because I am utterly besotted of Maud Gonne
I trapse around the Continent and these off-shore islands joining what she joins
Preaching revolution and resistance against the Empire
With let me say such approbation
That I have been elected President of the '98 Centennial Association
And President of the Wolfe Tone Memorial Committee
I do believe I am hot favourite to be chosen High King of a new Irish Workers' Republic !
Unemployed Irish Workers' Republic
[Laughter]

GONNE
Mr Connolly
I took the liberty of paying your fine
And found bail money for a few of the others
I hope I'm not wrong in thinking you are of more value out than in just now
....
Are you hurt ?
I saw you go down and feared the worst
To my shame I was inside the National Club when the police charged
Believe me I tried to get back out to be beside you
Someone locked the door and physically held me
I'll not say who
I shall never forgive him
My place was by your side
....
....
I think the people were magnificent
Everything

The meeting the march... dumping the coffin into the Liffey !
Ha ha ! It sank ! I was sure it would float
There wasn't a body in it was there ?
....
Just the remains of the British Empire
If you don't mind me saying so, Mr Connolly
I think you are the bravest man in Dublin
The only man who stood up to Queen Victoria and her henchmen
What is her Jubilee to us ?
Seventy years of shame
The figures you gave us last night... one-and-a-half million dead
Four-and-half million carted out in coffin-ships
Three million six hundred and sixty six thousand evictions was that it?
I fought against them as best I could
.....
It's no good pretending I'm a Marxist
I'm an old-fashioned nationalist
Maybe I shouldn't be in your party
But I love the poor people of Ireland
And find it hard to love the rich
Though I suppose relatively speaking I am one of them
But I would personally help hang every evicting landlord from his own doorpost

YEATS
You were magnificent
I felt so proud to walk beside you
At the head of your army of the poor
Head thrown back
You looked seven feet tall
The poor are so small

GONNE
Two things Willie
Your speech to the '98 meeting was excellent
You were at your very best in my opinion
The other thing your behaviour during the riot
Was a disgrace
I was thoroughly ashamed of you

YEATS
A woman was killed out there you know

GONNE
Mrs Fitzsimon
I would have saved her if I were on the street
A drunken policeman threw her off the car on the way to Jervis Street Hospital

YEATS
It's only because I love you I had to protect you

GONNE
If I want protection I'll get it from a man not a coward
Be as cowardly as ever you wish for yourself Willie
Which I happen to know you are not
But don't ever try to be a coward for me
You made me do the most cowardly act of my life last night
Sitting up there looking out at my comrades
Batoned beaten down left for dead or flung into carts like animals
People that we had led onto the streets of Dublin
...
Never will I work with you again
Never will I face physical danger with you
As long as I live

Now I must prepare myself for action in the West
There happens to be a famine in Co. Mayo
Savage evictions in Co. Roscommon

YEATS
I promised to spend a few days with Lady Gregory at Coole
I'm sure she'd be happy to have you stay there

GONNE
I'm sure she would not
Anyway it would be a bit of a joke
Fighting evictions all day
Then back to wine and dine in the manor house at Coole
Besides I've had quite enough of you

[EXEUNT to different spaces.
Light change.]

PART THREE

[THEY meet again.]

YEATS
I was driven to distraction
Hurt and worry

GONNE
I missed you Willie

YEATS
Expecting every day to hear the worst

GONNE
That's not what I hear
The life and soul of the party every night
Æ says

YEATS
At what a cost
Drugged up to the gills
It's not that I can't get a lover Maud
It seems I'm a hopeless monogamist

GONNE
I'm sorry dear

YEATS
You don't know what it's like for a young man
Such energy to get rid of
I walk write row around the lake like a demon
Compelled finally to masturbate in the most unlikely places
And that just makes me feel worse

GONNE
Lady Gregory is in love with you

YEATS
She is my good friend my sister my mother
She buys me clothes she lends me money
My lover no

GONNE
Lady Gregory marched into my rooms in Nassau Street last Monday morning
Demanded to know what were my intentions
Vis-a-vis the poet
'Fear not' says I ' Neither the poet nor I are the marrying kind'
She seemed relieved
Though not to the extent of having a cup of coffee
In the den of the lioness

YEATS
She encourages me to marry you

GONNE
She is quite handsome
In a dowdy sort of way
Is she related to Queen Victoria by any chance ?

YEATS
No idea

GONNE
How are your eyes Willie ?

YEATS
This one is getting worse

GONNE
They are so precious
Not burning the midnight candle I hope

YEATS
I do a bit of skyring
When I have someone psychic with me
Like you or Æ

GONNE
I had a very strong experience last night

YEATS
I have that every night

GONNE
I'm serious
I want to know if we shared something

YEATS
....
I dreamed of a kiss

GONNE
I saw several Celtic characters
Druids standing watch over me
Then the god Lugh appeared and took me with him
To a place full of spirits

YEATS
Just one kiss

GONNE
You were there

YEATS
You were dressed in a white robe

GONNE
Lugh took my hand and placed it in yours

YEATS
Like a bride

GONNE
I knew we were married
In a spiritual way

YEATS & GONNE
You kissed me

GONNE
And the vision went black

YEATS
You know in all the years you have never kissed me
With the bodily mouth

GONNE
I know
.....

[THEY come together and kiss passionately.]

YEATS
Maud we must marry

GONNE
No

YEATS
You love me

GONNE
No
Yes
I don't know Willie
You mean more to me than any man on earth

YEATS
That's near enough

GONNE
....
Remember the day on Howth Head ?

YEATS
Birds on the foam of the sea

GONNE
Yes

YEATS
Was that the first time I asked you to marry me ?

GONNE
I was called back to France

YEATS
The Boulanger gang
And then the little boy you took in died
I didn't see you for months

GONNE
The Boulanger group didn't call me back
The little boy...his name was Georges... do you remember ?

YEATS
Not the name

GONNE
Georges was my son

YEATS
I see
....
May I ask who the father is ?

GONNE
His father was a French politician...Julien Millevoye

YEATS
He called to your house when...
His house is it ?

GONNE
My house
We were sort-of lovers

YEATS
For how long ?

GONNE
Before I met you

YEATS
And now ?

GONNE
Not now
Though we still help each other politically
He has been a good friend to Ireland

YEATS
Who wouldn't
With Maud Gonne thrown in !

GONNE
So there
I had to tell you

YEATS
Why now ?
That must have been eight years back

GONNE
Something new was going on between us

YEATS
.....
My offer of marriage stands

GONNE
There's more

YEATS
Go on

GONNE
I can't tell you how much little Georges meant to me
I was a bad mother but I was a good mother too
Can you believe that ?
Oh such love as I gave the little fellow
He knew it and I knew it
We were going to be real friends as well until...
.....
I believed he could be reincarnated
You might not remember but Æ was certain about this
A child could be reincarnated in the same family...the same parents..

YEATS
Ah no !

GONNE
It had to be Julien
....
So I got him to have another child with me

YEATS
I don't believe this !

GONNE
Five years ago I had the second child

YEATS
But....how ?
When was this ?

GONNE
August

YEATS
I was in Paris with you in July

GONNE
You are not very observant
For a great poet

YEATS
And where do you...keep this son may I ask ?

GONNE
It is a daughter
Iseult
Quite a little beauty
She lives in my house in Paris
At present she is at school in the convent at Laval

YEATS
I do think you might have told me

GONNE
You haven't been very good at keeping secrets Willie
I have been surprised at some of the things that have come back to me

YEATS
So you haven't finished with what's-his-name Millevoye

GONNE
Political support I give him when I can
He needs that

YEATS
You never worry about what I need

GONNE
All the time

YEATS
I need time to think

GONNE
Time to talk it over with your friends at Coole Park

YEATS
.....
Will you marry me Maud Gonne

GONNE
Thank you Willie dear
Very gallant

YEATS
I mean it

GONNE
Marriage is not possible for me

YEATS

Life without you is impossible for me
We could adopt your little girl
Iseult you said ?
Thank you for telling me all this at last
It explains a lot of the seemingly inexplicable
Do you want to sleep on it ?

GONNE

It is out of the question

YEATS

Am I so unattractive ?

GONNE

It's very strange
I am physically attracted to you
And yet
I hardly want to touch you
You know how important you are to me
And I think I am to you
But I am afraid if I come too close
Something precious will crumble
Like a dream

YEATS

Kiss me like that just once more

GONNE

I should not have done it
I apologise

YEATS

I desperately need to make love with you
Married or not

GONNE

You should understand something else about me
Right I have had two children
Willie I have a horror and terror of the sexual act
I shriek like a tortured pig when I make myself do it

YEATS

I would be gentle as a girl

GONNE

The only justification I can see for sex
Is the need for a child
I don't have that need now
Oh god ! The cruel truth is if I did want another child
I'm not at all sure I would want a poet for its father
Forgive me
Quite a mess am I not ?

YEATS

....
It doesn't seem to matter to me what you are Maud
......

GONNE

I can live with myself

[A long silence.
Something starts to happen between them.
They enter into a spiritual marriage.]

GONNE
I hear the voice of Lugh
....
I am to have the initiation of the Thuatha de Danaan
The Cauldron

YEATS
The Sword

GONNE
The Stone

YEATS
The Spear
......
I come to you in my chariot
Touch you upon the breast with the spear

GONNE
I fall down upon the ground with a cry
And the fountain of fire plays over my body

YEATS
I hold the spear above your body

GONNE
I grasp the spear
And am raised erect by the fountain of fire
....
I am a great standing stone
Through which the fountain of fire might pass

YEATS
I am the burning flame
Mounting through the standing stone
I gaze out at the world
Through the eyes of the stone Minerva

GONNE
It is our mystical marriage
And will last forever

Part Four

GONNE
You'll never guess what I brought Iseult home from America

YEATS
I don't feel like playing guessing games any more

GONNE
A baby alligator
The nuns were horrified
They keep it in the fish pond
It has eaten all the goldfish

YEATS
I honestly think you are mad

GONNE
She loves animals

YEATS
No one can love an alligator Maud

GONNE
I can

YEATS
....
....
There's a rather bizarre joke going the rounds in Dublin
That you're marrying the McBride fellow

GONNE
Marriage is not a big thing Willie
He is a brave soldier
And might father a good warrior for me
For Ireland

YEATS
I am a coward
And would father cowards

GONNE
.....
You have a different kind of courage
It won't make any difference to our relationship

YEATS
It has driven me to seriously contemplate suicide
If that makes any difference

GONNE
The rather more important thing is
I have decided to become a Catholic

YEATS
Don't tell me any more
The whole thing is hilarious... Ha
.....
....
....
It's not at all hilarious
My real feelings are so extreme
I rarely express them even to you
In case I frighten you away

I who am so passive physically
Seethe inside with frightening violence
....
Maud in the name of fifteen years of friendship
In the name of our mystical marriage
Which you said would last forever...

GONNE
It will

YEATS
...In the name of the noble work
Appointed for us to undertake among the elite...

GONNE
The poor are the elite of Ireland
You are confused and seduced by wealth

YEATS
You are seduced by poverty and the cunning of the guttersnipe

GONNE
By whom ?

YEATS
It's a metaphor

GONNE
Liar
What guttersnipe seduced me ?

YEATS
All right...the Frenchman...Millevoye

Are you telling me his behaviour towards you
Was anything but that of a guttersnipe ?

GONNE
I was in love with him

YEATS
He promised to divorce his wife
Give your children a proper name
A proper home
Millevoye flaunted his new mistress in your house
Millevoye tried to sell your body to further his political ambitions

GONNE
I was in love with him

YEATS
Millevoye is a guttersnipe

GONNE
And now McBride ?

YEATS
I know nothing about McBride
But what I read in the papers
He is not a cultured man

GONNE
I weary of cultured men
McBride is a man of action
A hero of the Boer War against the British Empire
He will be a hero of the Irish war against the British Empire

YEATS
Ireland's war is against ignorance
Against the Philistines of Empire and Nationalism

GONNE
You've changed your tune

YEATS
All my life I have sought with you to know God
To know Truth
And just when I am getting close to something
You want to leave me

GONNE
I'll never leave you

YEATS
We are at a turning-point
You must choose the path of nobility
Or the path of baseness
Do not surrender your soul to the priest

GONNE
I believe in one god and one truth
Neither you nor the priest hold the whole truth
I was born into the Church of England
Into the army of Empire which my father served
Both of them I have to reject
My father was coming slowly to the same position
But he is dead
He saw the nobility of the Irish people he was paid to repress
Your big mistake is to confuse nobility with wealth and power
I see the nobility of the common people

The nursing mother watching her roof torn down by bailiffs
The prisoner unbroken by the savage jailer
I see that nobility of the poor
And the baseness of the powerful
I give myself to the masses
And because of some quality that God has given me
I become the voice of the masses
The very heart-beat of the masses
I stand beside the priest while the masses stand beside him

YEATS
The priest will always betray the people
He betrayed them at the Act Of Union
He denounced the Fenians from the altar of God
He betrayed Parnell
The priest will always hold back the people at the Gap of Danger

GONNE
I will be the first through the Gap of Danger
The people will follow me

YEATS
I appeal to you to come back to your real self

GONNE
You have taken the Saxon Shilling

YEATS
You are betraying your very soul

GONNE
I am the same woman you have known and loved

[MAUD GONNE turns
from him. THEY speak
overlapping but in
separate spaces..]

GONNE

I Edith Maud Gonne do take you John Patrick McBride
To be my lawful wedded husband
To have and to hold..........

YEATS

Lugh the great god of light placed your hand in mine
Bade us kiss with bodily mouth......
.....In sickness and in health
From this day forward....
And Lugh gave us a great task to accomplish together...
Till death us unite....

GONNE

....Till death us do part...
There was a ceremony to be gone through
In the British Embassy
Mc Bride who is still on the wanted list of course
Stood there with his finger on the trigger of his revolver

YEATS

....We were initiated of The Cauldron....

GONNE

....We spend our honeymoon in Spain
By order of the IRB
They sent us a little wedding gift
A silver salver

And asked for the head of King Edward VII...

YEATS
...We were initiated of The Stone....

GONNE
...Yes the young profligate was on a visit to Gibraltar
They ordered us to assassinate him ...

YEATS
...We were initiated of The Sword...

GONNE
...Neither the honeymoon nor the assassination
Could be described as a success
My little problem about sex has not gone away...

YEATS
...We were initiated of The Spear...
As for the killing of the King

GONNE
John McBride got involved with a couple of Irish lads he met in Algeciras
While King Edward was taking leave of the monkeys
On The rock of Gibraltar
Arrived back to our hotel drunk sometime after breakfast
Next morning

YEATS
My beloved alone understands
Yet she turns from me

GONNE
I gave McBride a piece of my mind

YEATS
When the world starts to praise my verse
Understanding nothing

GONNE
When he woke from his stupor
I was standing with my bags packed

YEATS
My beloved stands between me and every image

GONNE
Waiting for a taxi

YEATS
She is the hawk
She is the wren

GONNE
'I'm going home' I said

YEATS
She is the sun
She is the moon

GONNE
'You may come to me when you're sober '

YEATS
She is the deer

She is the mountain hare

GONNE
'You know I shall have to report this
To my IRB centre

YEATS
She is the slattern
She is the queen

GONNE
If he instructs me to shoot you
I'll do it

YEATS
She is the priest
She is the fool

GONNE
Nothing came of it
They make allowances for heroes
And drink

YEATS
She is the shield
She is the chariot

GONNE
Perhaps if I had been a better lover
He would have killed the King

YEATS
Maud King Edward didn't go to Gibraltar

Till two months after your marriage
April

GONNE
Our intelligence said he was there

YEATS
She is the salmon of knowledge
She is the wild swan on the lake

[Light change.]

Part Five

[Together in Dublin.]

YEATS
You should not have walked out !

GONNE
It is a horrible play

YEATS
You are Vice-President of the theatre
You betrayed me the theatre and the actors

GONNE
Synge betrays Irish womanhood !

YEATS
Ha ! That's a good one !

GONNE
Irish women are the most virtuous in the world

YEATS
That is not my experience

GONNE
You have no experience

YEATS
Is it yours ?
How is your little girl ?

GONNE
Thank you sir

YEATS
I'm sorry Maud
We're all sinners
Do you really think Ireland is the Island of Saints and Scholars ?

GONNE
It was
And will be again
And heroes
We are fighting for the very existence of the Irish race
Theatre is propaganda
It is for or it is against
There is no neutral ground

YEATS
Black and white is all right for a sketch
For a real picture you need colour and the half light

GONNE
Your *Cathleen ni Houlihan* has no half-light
No one walked out of that
The people understood it and supported it

YEATS
It is blatant propaganda
I wrote it to please you
I have to say I'm not very proud of that
I only hope no young man picks up a gun because of it

GONNE
I hope they do
And women

YEATS
Synge is the one genius in the entire Irish movement

GONNE
You are

YEATS
I don't know
I've tried to turn my pain
Into something useful
The pain of not having you

GONNE
I've tried to turn the pain
Of losing my father
Into something heroic
I haven't done very well

YEATS
You have done well

GONNE
In my life
There has been no moment of rest

YEATS
A few
When our love transcended the differences

GONNE

.....

Like now ?

YEATS

....

Like now

GONNE

....

Those moments don't last very long
What annoys me most about the Synge play
Is the way you foisted it on the company
And then expected me to sit through it like a dummy

YEATS

It was accepted by the Reading Committee

GONNE

It was accepted by half the Reading Committee
Over coffee in Lady Gregory's rooms
The anti-National clique you have trying to take over this theatre

YEATS

There is perhaps a clique
But it's not anti-National
It is pro Art

GONNE

Pro Willie Yeats
Annie Horniman is to buy you a new theatre isn't she
If you can get rid of the revolutionaries ?
Beware the Saxon Shilling Willie

Horniman hates the Irish particularly the Irish poor
Is it true she's making you double the price of the seats ?
That should keep the riff-raff out of your
Art-for-Art's-sake theatre eh ?
Her only virtue is that she is in love with you
Like Lady Gregory
Why on earth don't you marry one of them ?

YEATS
You had no right to marry
Without my agreement

GONNE
William Fay isn't in love with you but you seem to have him well under control
George Russell Douglas Hyde and Maud Gonne are to be by-passed, insulted
And presumably driven to resign

YEATS
You are extremely subversive

GONNE
What will you call the new theatre
'The Royal Horniman '?
Is that really her name ?
I think the sooner she marries the better
Is it true you're installing a special plush armchair for the British Chief Secretary ?
He is such a nice man

YEATS
It is customary

GONNE

What you have done is lure our Inghinidhe na hÉireann theatre
And the Fays' Irish Players into The National Theatre Society
Then pushed everyone out of the nest like a monstrous cuckoo
Don't worry dear, I'll resign quietly

YEATS

It might be a good idea

GONNE

And Russell and Douglas Hyde
Do you want me to ask them ?

YEATS

They'll go in their own time I think

GONNE

You don't want a theatre,
A theatre is essentially co-operative
You want a harem

YEATS

The truth is Maud I need to run the theatre my way
I haven't the time or patience to listen to the artistic theories
Of bricklayers and shop-girls

GONNE

Oh my god ! I never thought I'd hear this !
Let there be no mistake
I'm not resigning because I think you have any right to take over this company

This theatre was built on the inspiration and dedication and yes, artistic theories
And the pennies and sixpences of those same shop-girls and bricklayers
Who worked for this theatre mostly without wages after a ten-hour day in the sweatshops of Dublin
Not only are you stealing their theatre from them
You intend pricing them out of even watching the plays you put on here

YEATS
I always said our theatre was for the few not the many

GONNE
Yes but it was to be for the few who loved Ireland
And loved Ireland's myths stories and poetry

YEATS
That is still the position
But the context is broader
It is European it is universal

GONNE
You wanted to build me a Castle of Heroes on Lough Key
Where the young men of Ireland would gird themselves to bring Ireland her freedom

YEATS
I would still do it if you came with me

GONNE
I remember that island
And the stillness of the lake at twilight

On the shore, opposite the castle which is the castle of the McDermotts by the way
The English landlords who took over the McDermotts' lands
The King-Harman family... have built themselves a really pretty Regency manor house
An interesting feature of the house is that all the tradespeople...the shop-girls and bricklayers so to speak
Can only approach the house through long underground tunnels
So that the family in residence never have to offend their eyes
With the sight of the poor Irish trudging too and fro with their provisions
A bit like Miss Horniman's ideas for a high-class theatre is it not ?

YEATS
Husband or no husband
I'll still go to that island with you Maud

GONNE
No thank you
....
Oh by the way, I am six or seven months pregnant
You can hardly tell can you ?
John is over the moon about it and so am I
I always said children are the justification for marriage
And sex

[THEY EXIT to their separate spaces.]

YEATS
Your Excellency, Ladies and Gentlemen,
Today's battle is to be waged against the triple-headed Hydra of Irish ignorance

First there is the head of ill-informed Irish propaganda
Second there is the head of the ignorant priest
Who would deny all ideas
Not current among drovers at the nearest fair-green
The third Hydra-head is the head of the ignorant Irish politician
Who rejects every idea
Not immediately exchangeable for the votes of the innocent voter
......
So I would say Your Excellency Ladies and Gentlemen
The time for Anglophobia is long past
Hatred blunts the edge of imagination
There was a time when extremist politics in Ireland
Were the politics of intellectual liberation
But now under the flag of militant nationalism
And controlled by certain secret societies
The usually divided extremists have come together
In their mutual dislike of creative ideas....
...
It is time for Irish artists to look fearlessly
Into the depth of their own souls
For therein lies the only well-spring of great art
Great literature great theatre

GONNE
John McBride we must talk
...
Get yourself a drink if you have to
...
Not for me
....
I never promised to be an ordinary woman
I am a free agent
I sold my soul to the pagan gods

In exchange for my freedom
Does that frighten you ?
Well we are all Catholics now
So the old gods may go whistle for my soul
.....
There are a few things I need to say
I think our son Seán is magnificent
He is sufficient to justify the marriage
If you try to take him from me
I shall kill you
...
No. Since we became engaged
I have had no other lover
....
Any fool who says Seán is not your son
Should have his eyes examined
....
You have let me know often enough
I am a bad wife

.....
YOU MAY PACK YOUR BAGS AND GET OUT OF MY HOUSE RIGHT NOW !
.....
I think you know exactly what I am talking about
No I won't spell it out
But I tell you I'll wipe that smirk off your face
If you ever again in this life lay a hand on my daughter or my half sister
Or on that unfortunate housemaid
My God what were you thinking of John ?
Couldn't you go one of your twenty-Franc prostitutes if you were so desperate for sex ?

.....

This is all I have to say to you
I want you out of my house this night
I'll give you enough money
I want you to go to New York or Boston or somewhere in the United States
And stay there
You are the great Boer War hero over there and will have no problem getting employment
Which seems to elude you here
If you lead a decent life for a year or two
I will arrange for you to see your son from time to time
If that interests you

.....

I warn you do not try to take my son from me
I shall stop at nothing to keep him

....

...

Very well
We will fight it through the courts
I'll win John
If it takes me till the day I die

......

......

WILLIE HELP ME !

[YEATS and GONNE TOGETHER in Dublin.]

YEATS
The IRB sided with McBride

GONNE
Naturally
The man must be protected
Cumann na nGhaedheal elected him Vice President in place of me
Sinn Fein they're going to call it now

YEATS
Griffith always has a good word for you

GONNE
He tries to be fair
Like you
You were the best friend after all Willie

YEATS
I couldn't help it

GONNE
So in the end the court gave me nearly everything except a divorce
Because he is Irish

YEATS
Would you marry me if you got the divorce?

MAUD
I'm a Catholic
I take it quite seriously
...
I love you more than ever Willie

YEATS
Not me
I only love you exactly the same

GONNE
You know something ?
I'm feeling all funny inside
...
I think maybe I'm getting over the fear of sex

YEATS
You think so ?

GONNE
Yes
Yes I think so yes
.....

[A most tender embrace.
BLACKOUT. Pause.
A piercing scream in BLACKOUT. Pause.
Laughter in BLACKOUT.
Lights up on GONNE and YEATS hand in hand.]

GONNE
Ah my dearest one
I do love you

YEATS
It took us twenty years to find our way to that bed

GONNE
Some things shouldn't be rushed
......
Willie love

YEATS
Yes love ?

GONE

Sorry about the scream

YEATS

You were very courageous as usual

GONNE

After...just before I slept
I had a vision of Maeve and Ailill
In the stronghold at Rathcroghan
But it was us really
You...I mean Ailill came to me in my house
When I was combing my hair

YEATS

Your violent life has left no mark
Time has not touched your face

GONNE

We were united in some spiritual way
A sacrament but physical too
An ecstasy consumed my body
So I thought I would literally die from love

YEATS

Suffering has made you more noble
More ethereal

GONNE

I looked at you
You were radiant and more happy than I have ever seen you... Ailill

YEATS
Love has etched one line
Your children me Ireland

GONNE
That's three lines
....
We were dressed in spotless white robes
Like a transfiguration
Lit by Aillill's generations of love for Maeve

YEATS
You are more innocent
More child-like
Than you looked on that first day you came to see my father

GONNE
I told you
It wasn't your father I came to see
......
Our hands were joined like this
Above our heads
The voice of Ailill called out from far away
'It belongs to Ireland' and you did not understand
So I took it from you
And secreted it in the sacred hill at Rathcroghan
Until you had suffered enough...

YEATS
More than twenty years now

GONNE
...Now it is given back to you

It will last forever'

YEATS
You said you came to size me up
For Ireland

GONNE
A white bird flew out of your breast
And circled ever higher above us
Hush !
.....
.....
......
I heard a volley of shots

[MAUD GONNE runs swiftly from him.
Light change.]

Part Six

GONNE
Come here to me Seán
....
My you are grown up
Very smart
A real soldier of The Fianna
.....
....
Was Rory O'Connor there ?
....
Have you done the .303 ?
.....
Can you assemble it blindfold ?
......
I'm sure you are
I wanted to tell you something
I had a beautiful letter from a priest
Father Augustine...the Franciscan
He was with your father when they...
Yes
...
Your father was a very brave man Seán
They only executed the very bravest because they are the most dangerous
You'll have to learn the names of those brave men
And never forget them
I knew every one them
Remember Mr Connolly with the moustache ?
....
Yes he was
And poor old Tom Clarke the tobacconist

He used to say the cigarettes were killing him
Mr Pearse you knew better than I did
Wonderful poet and...
.....
Not as great a poet as Uncle Willie
But I suppose braver
In a way
McDonagh another poet...
Anyway do you want to know what Father Augustine says ?
And by the way Kevin O'Higgins who was in the next cell
Sent out a beautiful poem about your father
Though they never saw eye to eye on anything
He's making a copy for me
John McBride was the bravest of them all
When the soldiers came to take him out
They wanted to tie his hands behind his back
'Don't truss me up like a chicken' your father says
'I'll not run away from you'
'Sorry sir... orders is orders'
A soldier has to do what he's told right or wrong
Then the blindfold
'I don't need that' said John
And he called out to the lads in the other cells not to worry
'I've drunk strong tea in my day' he says
'And I've looked down the barrels of English guns often enough'
And he marched smartly out into the yard where the firing squad was waiting
Six standing six kneeling
With their 303s
The officer he pins a bit of white paper over John's heart
And nods to Father Augustine
Who leans over and whispers to John McBride
'John, offer up your death for all the sins of your past life'

Father Augustine was crying but McBride never flinched
'I'm glad you reminded me, Father'
Then the officer drew the priest away
There was no word spoken
Just a nod and the twelve guns rang out
......
And John McBride gave up his life for Ireland

[Light change.]

Part Seven

[Knocking at door.
Yeats opens it to an 'old woman'
She is bent double
head covered in a shawl.
It is Maud Gonne.]

YEATS
Yes ?

GONNE
A little help for the child sir
And god and His holy mother bless you sir

YEATS
I don't think I have any change...
My wife isn't very well just now...eh...

['Woman' straightens up
and throws back the shawl.]

GONNE
Aw come on Willie !
Just a few coppers ! Ha ha ha !

YEATS
Maud ! I...

GONNE
Are you going to leave me standing on the street ?

YEATS
I thought you were in Holloway Prison

GONNE
I'm out on parole
They told me not to leave London but...
Have a look will you dear ?
I think maybe my cab was followed from the Mailboat

YEATS
...
I don't know Maud
Is that your cab outside ?
My eyesight isn't the best

GONNE
Let me see
I hoped with an election coming up
The Police might turn a blind eye

YEATS
Have you eaten ?
I'll see if the cook is downstairs

GONNE
I'm not at all hungry
I'll bring in Iseult and Seán
If the street is clear

YEATS
Where are you staying ?

GONNE
Here if that's all right with your wife

YEATS
George is recovering from pneumonia
She's expecting a child in a couple of months

GONNE
Is she up ?
I should have a word w...

YEATS
I think she's asleep
...
Maud dear I think it would not be a good idea to stay here

GONNE
Whatever you say Willie
I'll start looking for a house tomorrow

YEATS
Where will you stay tonight ?

GONNE
You don't want us here even for one night ?

YEATS
A police raid in the middle of the night
Would be really serious for Georgie

GONNE
I thought...
I mean it is my house my dear

YEATS
You can't have it both ways Maud
I rented the house from you to help you out

GONNE
I know all that
Are you turning me away from your door ?

YEATS
The Nassau is just round the square
You always liked it there

GONNE
Give the police credit for some glimmer of intelligence
Where is the first place they'd look for me ?

YEATS
Here

GONNE
I don't think so
Look I can't leave Seán and Iseult out there in the freezing cold

YEATS
I think it's utterly irresponsible
First of all breaking your parole or whatever it is
And then... going on the run like a common criminal
With your children in tow

GONNE
They are not children
....

You are an unmitigated coward Yeats

YEATS
I have a responsibility to my pregnant wife

GONNE
I though you were my truest friend

YEATS
If you were my wife I'd face Hell for you

GONNE
'Wife' ! What has 'wife' got to do with our relationship ?
....
You wanted to build a castle of heroes for me on Lough Key
Heroes !
You'd dump me into the lake if the local peeler showed his face within a mile
Of our castle of heroes !
At least I had the wit not to let a coward father my child
McBride was vindicated at the end of all

YEATS
Because I am not an outlaw
Does not mean I am a coward
If we lose this child we may never have another
I am a bit beyond playing Wild West games with you and the police
And putting my liberty and my wife's health in jeopardy into the bargain

GONNE
Is it true you refused a knighthood Willie ?

YEATS
Yes

GONNE
Why ever did you do that ?
After all the English made you
And your theatre what you are

[EXEUNT each to their own space.]

Part Eight

[Union Jack down.
Tricolour flies over Ireland.
GONNE and YEATS in Dublin.]

GONNE
Your Free State Government is painting the post-boxes green

YEATS
It's a start

GONNE
You have twelve thousand republicans locked up
In jails and concentration camps
Without trial or charge
I was released because your police believed I was about to die in Kilmainham Jail

YEATS
I did every thing humanly possible to get you out

GONNE
You voted to put me in, Senator Yeats
You voted for O'Higgens's Public Safety Act
You voted for the Flogging Bills
You voted for the Treason Bills

YEATS
Yes I did
It would have been easier to stay down in the country
After much heart-searching I voted for strong government

GONNE
You used to be a republican

YEATS
That's right
My reading of Balzac changed my politics
Create...hate no man
And Neitzche
Dictatorship of the intellectual elite
It's what Europe needs right now

GONNE
You are afraid of the poor
I love them

YEATS
You love the idea of the poor rebelling
You love the idea of Ireland
I love the reality the very turf and rocks
And the people
It's like our sexual relationship
For you the mystical ideal union
For me physical union
Our political and sexual differences haven't changed
Since the day we met

GONNE
Your republicanism has changed

YEATS
My republicanism was a station on a long journey

GONNE
I was a wayside station

YEATS
A journey round Maud Gonne
Never reached never abandoned

GONNE
My entire family is interned
Iseult...her husband...my son

YEATS
I thought Seán had escaped

GONNE
Kevin O'Higgins promised me Seán would not be arrested
That promise was not honoured
Seán is back in Mountjoy

YEATS
A murdered man honours no promises

GONNE
They have charged Seán with the..execution of O'Higgins

YEATS
Ah !

GONNE
He was a hundred miles away and can prove it
But under this extraordinary Public Safety Act of yours
One of your acts of strong government
Anyone...you me Seán... as he knows to his cost...

Can be arrested and charged
With the most heinous crimes
Imprisoned flogged deported shot
But he can never be acquitted
A nightmare of a law is it not

YEATS
Civil war is a national nightmare

GONNE
The reason I came to see you
As my best friend
Is Seán.....

YEATS
I'll talk to Cosgrave

GONNE
Do that
But.....
Willie we are going to spring Seán out of Mountjoy
I have to trust you with this
.....
I'm setting up a few safe houses
Where we can leave Seán for a week or two
Till we move him out of the country

YEATS
You shouldn't tell me this

GONNE
I'm only telling the people who have the safe houses

YEATS
Not me

GONNE
I'm asking you this Willie
To do this one thing for me

YEATS
Let me think for a moment
....
....
....
Maud this is what I will say to you
I have elected to take an oath of loyalty to this new state
With all its failings
I can not be party to a treasonable act
You should not have asked me do such a dishonourable thing
I will forget what you have said to me
But do not speak about such things to me again
It is quite out of the question

GONNE
What is it about me
That generates such loyalty from my men friends
You shut your door on me when I was on the run from the British
You swore no oath of loyalty to them I presume
My other good friend Arthur Griffith
Remember he used to say we were his two best friends ?
Griffith shut his door in my face when I went to him
After the Mulcahy and Collins gang shelled the Four Courts
Seán was inside of course
I led a deputation of The Women's Peace Committee
Trying to broker a truce

He barred the door of his office like this...
'Women should stay out of politics' he shouted at me
'Get her out !'
When you think of what women did for Irish politics...for
Griffith...for you
Griffith was dead within the month

YEATS
He died of a broken heart

GONNE
He died of broken promises

YEATS
When I met you feeding the school-children
...Was that in the 1913 lock-out ?
You told me all your troubles came from involvement in movements
driven by hate

GONNE
We all have moments of self-doubt
Driven by hate sometimes but more by love
I have worked for Irish prisoners from 1888 right to the present day
That was a long act of love
The evictions the '98 commemoration the Wolfe Tone Memorial
Every single thing I have done with you has been an act of love
My family
The meals for Dublin's poor children
Innghinidhe na hEireann...Cumann nGaedheal
Amnesty
Don't ever accuse me of not loving enough Willie

YEATS

....

.....

.....

Everything ...almost everything I have done in my life
Has been for me
Everything you have done has been for others

GONNE

We can't afford to have our national poet
Succumb to self-doubt

YEATS

A momentary lapse. Ha ha !

GONNE

Your new book arrived
I love it
I really like you setting me among children
It's where I was happiest after all
Except....
Someone is calling me

[GONNE draws her revolver
and walks out without hesitation.
She returns quickly.]

GONNE

It's about Seán...
They have abandoned his trial
They have released him
Without condition without explanation
He will be home for his supper
Goodbye Senator Yeats

YEATS

Maud !

Let me take care of that gun for you

GONNE

....

....

Thank you Willie

YEATS

They shot Erskine Childers for one smaller than this

....

Maud we are having a few people round to lunch tomorrow
Any chance of you joining us ?

GONNE

What day of the week is it ? Sunday
No dear. Every Sunday I hold a vigil on O'Connell Street

YEATS

Every Sunday ?

GONNE

Only till the last political prisoner is released

[MAUD GONNE is walking out.]

YEATS

You are a fool Maud Gonne
A wonderful wonderful fool

....

END OF THE PLAY

www.ingramcontent.com/pod-product-compliance
Ingram Content Group UK Ltd.
Pitfield, Milton Keynes, MK11 3LW, UK
UKHW012240240726
13966UKWH00003B/1184

9 781847 537652